HOW MOUNTAIN GORILLAS LIVE

BY VIRGINIA HARRISON • PHOTOGRAPHY BY MICHAEL NICHOLS

Gareth Stevens Children's Books
MILWAUKEE

A note from the publisher: Today, the existence of the mountain gorilla is limited to one region on earth — the rain forests of central Africa's Virunga volcanoes. Through conservation efforts and educational programs, the mountain gorilla has a chance for continued survival. We hope that books like this one will help young readers appreciate the value of a species and its natural right to live alongside humankind.

For a free color catalog describing Gareth Stevens' list of high-quality children's books, call 1-800-341-3569 (USA) or 1-800-461-9120 (Canada).

Library of Congress Cataloging-in-Publication Data

Harrison, Virginia, 1966-
    How mountain gorillas live / by Virginia Harrison ; photographs by Michael Nichols.
      p. cm. -- (Animal world)
    Includes bibliographical references and index.
    Summary: Introduces the eating habits, social organization, and daily routine of the mountain gorillas of Africa's Virunga volcanoes.
    ISBN 0-8368-0446-5
    1. Gorilla--Juvenile literture. 2. Gorilla--Virunga--Juvenile literature. [1. Gorilla.] I. Nichols, Michael, ill. II. Title. III. Series: Animal world (Milwaukee, Wis.)
    QL737.P96H378   1991
    599.88'46--dc20   91-2022

A Gareth Stevens Children's Book edition

Edited, designed, and produced by
Gareth Stevens Children's Books
1555 North RiverCenter Drive, Suite 201
Milwaukee, Wisconsin 53212, USA

How Mountain Gorillas Live is based on the book *Gorillas*, by Michael Nichols and George Schaller, originally published by Aperture Foundation, Inc. Aperture publishes a periodical, books, and portfolios of fine photography to communicate with serious photographers and creative people everywhere. A complete catalog is available upon request. Address: Aperture, 20 East 23 Street, New York, NY 10010.

Series editor: Rita Reitci
Series and cover design: Laurie Shock
Book design: Kate Kriege

Printed in the United States of America

1 2 3 4 5 6 7 8 9 97 96 95 94 93 92 91

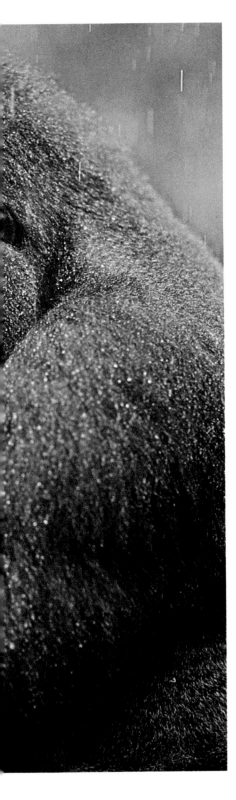

CONTENTS

Words in **bold type** are explained in the glossary.

Mountains Are Home

High up in the **rain forests** of the Virunga volcanoes live the mountain gorillas. Only about 400 of these animals are still in existence, and their home is among six inactive volcanoes in central Africa.

Mountain gorillas **forage** on the steep volcanic slopes. Gorilla families wander in search of the plants they live on. They enjoy **bamboo** shoots, vines, the leaves of nettles and thistles, and many other plants.

This **blackback** gorilla is foraging for his favorite plants. ▼

▲ Looking through the giant heather that grows on the slopes of the Virunga volcanoes.

Parts of Zaire, Rwanda, and Uganda (area shown in red on map above) border the Virunga volcano range, home to mountain gorillas (green on map to right). ▶

UGANDA

Lake Kivu

ZAIRE

RWANDA

TANZANIA

BURUNDI

Peaceful Gorillas

Gorillas belong to the **primates** group, along with monkeys and humans. Though fierce-looking, gorillas are gentle animals living in family groups.

Their mountain home is cool and damp. So mountain gorillas have thicker hair than **lowland gorillas**. In this book, we will follow the daily lives of one mountain gorilla family.

The gorillas usually wake up at dawn. After yawning and stretching, they follow their leader through the forest in search of food.

▲ A gorilla yawning. The gorilla's teeth are flat and full of black tartar, showing that they eat plants. Meat-eaters have sharp teeth.

◀ The close of another day. The **silverback** leader takes his family group on its last foraging trip before nesting for the night.

A silverback peacefully enjoying the sunshine. Many gorilla actions remind us of human ways. ▶

This blackback gorilla is watching for enemies. Blackbacks are adult males between eight and twelve years old.

A gorilla family group may have around 15 members. They remain a close-knit group through many generations. ▼

A Gorilla Family

The group's leader is a big gorilla with silver hair on his back. This silverback decides where the family travels and when they eat and sleep. He is the father of the young, and he protects his family from harm.

The silverback leads a band of four females with **infants**, several youngsters, and two adult males that are not old enough to have silver hair. They are blackbacks, and they help guard the family.

After the age of twelve, male gorillas begin to grow silver fur on their backs. Then they look for a female mate, so they can form a new family group. ▶

◀ A gorilla's hand is flexible like a human hand. It has fingers, fingernails, and a thumb. A silverback's hand can be six inches (15 cm) wide.

Plants to Eat

The gorillas find a good feeding place. Most of them sit down and begin eating. Some climb into trees to gather fruit or eat the ferns growing on the branches.

Using their big teeth and strong jaws, gorillas peel celery stems or the bark from branches and eat the inside. They break off stems and branches with their powerful arms. Their **flexible hands** pick buds and leaves.

After a while, they move on to find another feeding place.

◄ This silverback cracks open tough bamboo stalks with his strong jaws and teeth.

◄ Gorillas, monkeys, and humans can pick up small objects with their thumb and fingers.

11

More Foods

The gorillas like rare treats, such as the **fungus** on trees and certain kinds of fruits. They also eat ant eggs and grubs. To get the minerals they need, they sometimes eat dirt.

The family never has to search for water. Rain and dew collect on the leaves, and many plants are juicy. This is enough for the gorillas. Mothers **nurse** their infants on their milk.

A WATER ZONE
During the drier months, gorillas move to the giant lobelia zone. This region is higher than their usual **feeding range**. The plants there hold on to the night's moisture, and the gorillas get their water from them.

◀ While this gorilla eats, he is also getting water that clings to the leaves and juice from inside the plant.

New bamboo shoots are a favorite food. Gorillas travel to the bamboo areas in the season when the shoots begin to grow. ▶

Letting Others Know

In the thick growth, gorillas may grunt to tell others where they are. Gorillas also bark and scream in warning, rumble in relaxation, and roar in anger.

Gorilla actions also have meaning. A gorilla shaking its head means no harm. A gorilla crouching down with arms and legs tucked under is giving in to another. A gorilla can show power by staring. One silverback showing his strength to another will make a big display of slapping his hands on his chest.

GORILLA SOUNDS
Gorillas are usually quiet animals. But they can make 25 different sounds that range from hooting to chuckling. A silverback hooting to warn off other males can be heard for a mile through the forest. But he will chuckle playfully when he relaxes with his family group.

◀ If looks could kill! This staring silverback is using a nonviolent way of showing he is in charge.

This silverback feels threatened by the arrival of another strong male. His chest-slapping and loud screams scare the visitor away. ▶

Midday Rest

After about two hours of roaming and feeding, the gorillas rest. The adults take naps, sometimes lying in nests they've made or sitting against trees. The youngsters race, climb, wrestle, or play follow-the-leader.

A mother reaches out when her infant moves too far away. A young female borrows a baby to practice caring for it. Two blackbacks **groom** each other, picking insects and dirt from each other's hair and skin.

Finally, it's time to move on to another feeding place.

▲ When the silverback (left) begins napping, the other adults soon follow. During the midday rest, most of the gorillas make nests on the ground.

◀ A female sprawls in the sun on the leafy nest she has made.

While mom sleeps, her youngest offspring nurses from her breasts. Gorilla young are weaned at three years of age. ▼

▲ The silverback awakens and sits up. Soon, the rest of the group will rise and move on.

17

Nesting at Night

At the end of the day, the silverback stops for the night. He is big and heavy, so he makes his nest on the ground. The others may build their nests in trees or on the ground.

A mother gorilla sits in the fork of a tree. She pulls in small branches and bends them around her in a circle. She shoves the tips under her body. When her nest is finished, her baby creeps in to sleep beside her.

▲ This youngster is looking for a nesting place in a Hagenia tree. These large, mossy trees make good places for sleeping.

◀ This silverback is too heavy to nest in trees. He can also sense danger quicker from the ground.

These youngsters practice
nest-building by bending
vines and branches
inward. ▶

Meeting Other Gorillas

In the morning, the silverback leads his family farther along their feeding range. Later, they meet another gorilla group. For a while, the youngsters play together. But the adults just keep on feeding.

Then one of the silverback's **mates** moves into the other group. This is one way a gorilla leader can enlarge his group. The silverback grunts for his mate to come back. But the leader of the other group will not let her go.

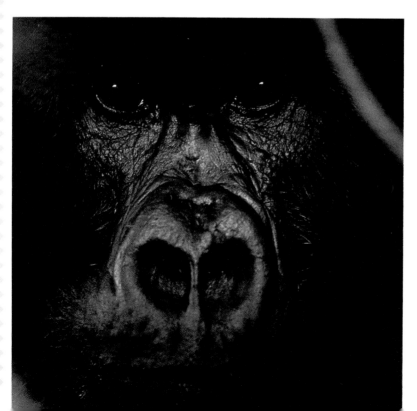

◀ The family's silverback has just lost one of his mates to the other group.

▲ As the family forages in
its chosen feeding area,
another gorilla group arrives.

When threatened, a silver-back may go through a series of noises and actions to show another silver-back how strong he is. Here, a silverback begins with loud hooting. ▶

This fierce-looking silver-back roars as he slaps his hands loudly on his chest. ▶

A Show of Power

The family's silverback shows off his strength. He begins hooting louder and louder. He rises up on his legs and throws some plants into the air. He slaps his chest with his hands. He kicks up his leg.

Then the silverback rushes on both legs toward the other group's leader. While running, he rips off leaves and branches. Then he beats the ground with his palms in front of the other silverback.

As males grow, they practice the displays of strength that they have seen silverbacks perform. Here an adult male — still a blackback — rushes at an opponent, tearing at plants and tree branches as he runs. ▶

◄ The other silverback wants to keep the new female in his group. He stares in warning at the family's silverback.

How Gorillas Win

The other group's leader **struts** up and down before the family's silverback. He shakes tree branches. He screams and shows his sharp teeth.

Then the two silverbacks put their faces very close. They stare for a long time. Finally, the other leader gives up and turns away. The family's silverback takes his mate back to their own group.

Gorillas sometimes fight each other. But they would rather win by scaring the other one away.

◄ The family's silverback stares back at the other group's leader. He will not give up.

The family's silverback shows threatening teeth. At last, the other silverback gives up and leads his group away. ▶

New Gorilla Families

A female gorilla can have her first baby when she is about eight years old. But a young female usually mates with a male from another family group.

A male gorilla becomes a silverback after he is twelve years old. Then he usually leaves his family group to find a mate. The two will then start their own family.

Two adult gorillas and their infant — the start of a new family. In time, more young females will join this group and begin having babies.

27

Gorillas at Peace

For several days, a single young silverback has been following the family. He shakes his head to show he means no harm. One of the family's daughters is old enough to mate. When the young silverback wanders away, she goes with him.

Later, the family's silverback nests for the night. He lets one of his mates groom him. Tomorrow he will lead his family to where the bamboo shoots grow. He rumbles peacefully and falls asleep.

◀ The silverback is content. He and his family have eaten, played, traveled, and slept today as they do every day.

▲ The sun sets over the Virunga volcanoes. Tomorrow, the family will awaken to begin another day.

Gorilla Facts

A gorilla's hand is twice the size of a human hand. A gorilla's foot is a little longer than a human foot, but it is much wider.

All primates, including gorillas, originally lived in trees. Today, gorillas spend most of their time on the ground. They only climb trees to look for food or to sleep at night. Most silverbacks are so big that they can't climb and have to sleep on the ground!

Female gorillas never get pregnant until their last baby is old enough to take care of itself. This usually happens when the baby is about three years old.

Most of the volcanoes in the Virunga mountains have not erupted in many years. Only two of the eight volcanoes are still active. The gorillas stay away from those volcanoes.

More Books to Read

Here are more books about gorillas. If you would like to read them, look in your library, or ask an adult to order them for you at a bookstore.

Games Gorillas Play. Darling and Freed (Garrard)
Gorilla. Brown (Knopf)
Gorillas and Chimps. Chivers (Gloucester)
Gargantua: The Mighty Gorilla.
    Glendinning and Glendinning (Garrard)
In the Jungle. Booth (Raintree)
Koko's Kitten. Patterson (Scholastic)
Koko's Story. Patterson (Scholastic)
Monkeys and Apes. Barrett (Watts)
Mountain Gorillas and Their Young.
    Harrison (Gareth Stevens)
Mountain Gorillas in Danger.
    Ritchie (Gareth Stevens)
Patti's Pet Gorilla. Mauser (Macmillan)
Rain Forest. Coucher (Farrar, Straus & Giroux)

Places To Write

If you would like to find out more about gorillas and how they live, the groups listed below can help you. When you write, be sure to say exactly what you want to know. Always include your full name, address, and age, and enclose a stamped envelope addressed to yourself.

Gorilla Foundation
P.O. Box 620-530
Woodside, California 94062

Rainforest Action Network
301 Broadway, Suite A
San Francisco, California
   94133

The Mountain Gorilla
   Project
African Wildlife Foundation
1717 Massachusetts
   Avenue, NW, Suite 602
Washington, DC 20036

World Wildlife Fund
   (Canada)
90 Eglindon Avenue E,
   Suite 504
Toronto, Ontario M4P 2Z7

Glossary

Bamboo: A grass with hollow stems that grows up to 100 feet (30 m) tall. Bamboo is a favorite food of gorillas.

Blackback: An adult male gorilla that is between eight and twelve years old. His back hair will not turn silver until he is about twelve years old and ready to mate. Then he will leave his family group to look for a mate. Meanwhile, he helps to protect his group.

Feeding range: The area through which a family group of gorillas will roam on its daily search for food. Often several family groups will share overlapping ranges. This is one way that gorilla groups meet.

Flexible hands: Hands and fingers easily able to bend. Because their hands are so flexible, gorillas are able to do a lot of things with them. One gorilla, given a magazine, was able to turn the pages!

Forage: To get or take food. Gorillas eat most of the time that they are not sleeping.

Fungus (*plural***: fungi):** A plantlike growth that thrives wherever it is warm and wet. Mushrooms and toadstools are common kinds of fungus. Some fungi grow on trees.

Groom: To comb by hand Gorillas spend a lot of time grooming each other, carefully removing fleas, twigs, and burrs from one another's fur.

Infant: A baby gorilla under three years old. Infants stay close to their mothers because they are unable to feed and protect themselves.

Lowland gorilla: The most common of the three kinds of gorillas living today. Lowland gorillas live in West Africa. The mountain gorilla is the rarest gorilla. The third kind is Grauer's gorilla, living in central Africa. The gorillas you see in zoos are lowland gorillas. There is no mountain gorilla in any zoo, because it cannot survive in captivity.

Mate: To pair off a male and a female gorilla in order to have babies. Usually all the adult females in a family group will be mates of the silverback, and all the infants will be his children.

Nurse: To drink milk from the breast of one's mother.

Primate: A member of the animal group that includes humans, gorillas, and monkeys. Primates are considered the most intelligent creatures on this planet. They can adjust to new things and changes around them very easily.

Rain forest: A thick forest or jungle that gets at least 70-100 inches (about 180-250 cm) of rain a year. Most rain forests are located in the tropics. These forests have the greatest number of different kinds of plants of any habitat.

Silverback: A full-grown male gorilla at least twelve years old. A silverback leads each gorilla family. He protects the group and is the father of the infants. He is called a silverback because of the silver hairs on his back.

Strut: To walk boldly back and forth, showing off.

Index